The Monster in the  Washer

(and the Disappearing Socks)

Written by Kelly Hufnagle Miller
Illustrated by Paul Cox

ylon Henry,
I'm sure you are a
"monster" of an author,
too!
Kelly

www.KellMeAStory.com
KellMeAStory@gmail.com
www.facebook.com/
TheMonsterInTheWasher

AuthorHouse™
1663 Liberty Drive
Bloomington, IN 47403
www.authorhouse.com
Phone: 1-800-839-8640

Published by AuthorHouse 7/25/2012

ISBN: 978-1-4772-5187-4 (sc)
ISBN: 978-1-4772-5186-7 (e)

Library of Congress Control Number: 2012913400

Any people depicted in stock imagery provided by Thinkstock are models,
and such images are being used for illustrative purposes only.
Certain stock imagery © Thinkstock.

This book is printed on acid-free paper.

Because of the dynamic nature of the Internet, any web addresses or links contained in this book may have changed since publication and may no longer be valid. The views expressed in this work are solely those of the author and do not necessarily reflect the views of the publisher, and the publisher hereby disclaims any responsibility for them.

authorHOUSE®

To Brandon, Mom, Dad, Britany, and my family and friends for all the support, encouragement, and belief in this first book, and all those to come- a truly heartfelt thank you. To those ethereal, most sincere appreciation for all the abundance imaginable. For those children who have touched my life in our classroom and told me their sweet stories, this time I'll tell you mine.

**Rumble!
Grumble!
Snarl!
Tumble!**

Did you hear that?
'Thought you might!
Something scary,
full of fright!

Not only is it noisy,
and very impolite,
It's a MONSTER! In the WASHER!
He eats my socks up every night!

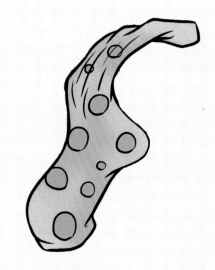

Mommy puts them in the washer,
from up off of the floor.
They go down deep inside,
and they're lost forever more.

I'm sure that there's a monster,
and his hunger's hard to beat.
He's ooey, gooey, drooling,
for the warmers of my feet!

When mommy dumps the basket,
into the washer's drum,
I'm sure the socks go in there,
and that monster, he says, "YUM!"

She adds in all the soap,
and closes up the lid.
But deep inside the washer,
is where that monster hid!

As soon as water's spinning,
he now begins his feast.
And there goes my toes' favorite things,
now eaten by this beast!

Blue, striped, red, or silly,
short, tall, polka dots, or white,
as the washer's banging,
he gulps them in one bite!

Heels... CHOMP!

Toes... SLURP!

And when the washer's done, and "beeped,"

I thought I heard a BURRRRRP!

Mommy brought the basket,
to take them to the line.
She searched and then she scoured,
for the socks that were just mine.

She reached down in
and swished around.
And what do you think,
that she found?

One purple sock,
one fuzzy sock,
and one with stars that glow.

One heel chewed off,
one gnawed in half,
and one without the toe!

Now, mommy she just looked at me,
with quite a puzzled look.
She lifted up her finger,
and then, her head, it shook.

"I don't know where your socks went,"
said mommy very gruff,
"But when I learn the story,
I will be very tough."

"Our monster in the washer,
I know he has to eat.
But other things are good for him,
and don't go on your feet!"

She leaned in deep and looked around,
then stood up tall and proud.
She shut the lid up with a "BANG!"
Her voice got very LOUD.

"The monster in our washer,
he's full up to the brim.
And the socks that you were missing...
were stuck under the rim."

She handed me my socks,
with the pieces that were ripped.
And when she turned to walk away,
I swear...the lid... it tipped!

About the Author

Kelly Hufnagle Miller has spent the better part of the last decade teaching kindergarten using her certifications in Early Childhood Education, Elementary Education, and English as a Second Language (ESL). Based on her experiences, she has lots of story ideas for years to come! In her time out of the classroom she is assisted in her piles of laundry by her husband, Brandon, and their two rescue dogs, Lincoln and Maggie. They all live in central Pennsylvania, and so far, only four dog blankets have been lost to the monster in their washer.